Early Prevention Series

THE CHEETAH WHO LOST HER SPEED
A Story About Staying Fit

by Marcia Shoshana Nass
illustrated by Steve Harpster

Childswork ChildsPLAY™
A Brand of Sunburst Visual Media

THE CHEETAH WHO LOST HER SPEED

A Story About Staying Fit
by Marcia Shoshana Nass
illustrated by Steve Harpster

Childswork/Childsplay publishes products for mental health professionals, teachers, and parents who wish to help children with their developmental, social, and emotional growth.
For questions and comments, call 1-800-962-1141.

© 2006 Childswork/Childsplay
A Brand of Sunburst Visual Media
P.O. Box 9120
Plainview, NY 11803-9020

ISBN 1-58815-067-4

Introduction

Childhood obesity has become a major physical and mental health problem for American children. Besides the serious health risks of being overweight, obese children almost always have low self-esteem, which can contribute to problems in making friends and predispose them to academic underachievement.

The best way to prevent childhood obesity is to begin teaching children the value of a healthy lifestyle at an early age and to keep repeating this message throughout their childhood and into adolescence. Of course, teaching children to make good choices is just the beginning. We can help them develop healthy lifestyles by making sure that they have healthy meals and snacks, by scheduling at least an hour of exercise each day, and by limiting their time in front of the TV. And we can make the most impact simply by being good role models.

This book tells the story of Coco the Cheetah, who loses her speed after developing the bad habits of eating junk food and watching too much TV. Fortunately she learns to make good choices about her eating and exercise habits, and she becomes a star athlete again. It is designed to reinforce the importance of developing a healthy lifestyle and to help children resist the temptations all around them.

The Childswork/Childsplay Early Prevention Series is designed to help young children learn about common emotional and behavioral problems and acquire skills that can help prevent these problems from becoming serious. Learning to eat right and exercise will affect every aspect of a child's development. They are habits that should be talked about and reinforced every day.

-Lawrence E. Shapiro, Ph.D.

Activity Sheet

The *Coco* doll that comes with this book can be used to help reinforce the lessons of *The Cheetah Who Lost Her Speed*. You can use the doll with the following play activities to teach and reinforce the importance of having a healthy lifestyle.

Role Play

The adult can narrate the story and the child, using the doll, can take the role of Coco. After the story, take time to ask the child questions, such as:

"What do you think about the things that you eat? Do you think that they are good for you?"

"Do you watch too much TV? How do you know when someone watches too much TV?"

"Who do you know that has good eating and exercise habits? What do they do?"

Make Up a Story or Play

You can also encourage children to make up their own story or play, using Coco with other dolls or stuffed animals. For example, Coco could teach other animals the lessons she has learned about good eating and exercise habits.

You may also want to make a videotape of the dolls acting out a story, which the child can then watch. Viewing positive scenes can help the child internalize the messages of the book.

Use the Doll as a Reminder of the Importance of a Healthy Lifestyle

Young children often attribute magical powers to their toys. A child may want to have the Coco doll as a playmate or bedtime companion. Just having the doll can serve as a reminder that children need to take care of their bodies so that that they can grow up to be happy and healthy.

Coco the Cheetah loved to run. She ran in all kinds of weather. She was so speedy that on a rainy day she could run between raindrops and not get a bit wet.

Coco was the youngest member of the Nambia Elementary School track team. She was only seven years old, and she could already run faster than her father. She could run faster than her mother. She could even run faster than her older brother, Chaz.

Today Mr. Phil, the track team coach, was planning to time the cheetahs to see how fast they could run.

"The Jungle Races are four months away, and today is our first official practice. Whoever wins the final race when the judges come in May will represent our school."

"I'll be cheering for you," said Coco's best friend, Charlie. Mr. Phil told the cheetahs to take their places at the starting line. He blew his whistle, and the cheetahs took off.

"Go, Coco, go," yelled Charlie from the stands. He watched as Coco ran so fast that she seemed to almost fly. The other cheetahs were way behind, and Coco reached the finish line first.

"Hip, hip, hooray!" shouted Charlie.

Mr. Phil looked at his watch and smiled. "Nice going, Coco. You ran that track in record time. If you keep it up, you'll be the one to run at the Jungle Races."

As all the other cheetahs looked on, Mr. Phil added, "You're our own Little Speedy."

Coco rushed home to tell her mom and dad.

"It's all over town," said Dad. "You broke a record. They said the track coach calls you Little Speedy." He took out a present for Coco.

Coco unwrapped a shirt that said "Born to Run" in big letters across the front.

"Does it fit?" asked Dad.

Coco held it against her. "It's perfect," she said. She gave her dad a kiss.

Mom came out from the kitchen. "Come over here, you cute Little Speedy," she said and hugged Coco proudly. "In honor of your special day, I made chocolate cake for dessert." She held out a huge chocolate cake.

"That looks mighty good," said Dad.

"Yum, yum, yummy," said Chaz, patting his stomach.

But when it was time for dessert, Coco was full.

"But you have to have a piece of cake," said her mom. "I made it specially for you."

Coco had a piece of cake.

"Oh, Coco, have another. Just a tiny slice. You did so well today," her mom said, as she cut Coco another slice of cake.

Coco had to admit that the cake tasted good. But after the second slice, she felt too full and sleepy to go for her evening run. Instead, she stayed in and watched television.

The next morning on their way to school, Coco and Charlie passed a building with lots of balloons and colorful signs. A big banner announced that a Cheetah Queen was opening!

"Wow, Cheetah Queen. My cousin has a Cheetah Queen where she lives. Want to go after school?" Charlie asked.

"I have to run. I missed my run last night, and this morning I felt so sleepy that I didn't make it up," answered Coco.

"But everyone will be going to Cheetah Queen this afternoon. You can run later," coaxed Charlie.

"Okay," Coco agreed. "Cheetah Queen it is."

After school, Coco and Charlie went straight to Cheetah Queen.

"Sit here," called Oliver and Carla, two cheetahs from their class.

"What will it be?" asked the waitress.

"I'll have what they're having," said Charlie.

"I had a big salad for lunch. I'm not that hungry," said Coco.

"You've got to taste the super-deluxe burger and the fries," said Oliver.

"Well ... okay," said Coco. She wasn't really hungry, but once she started eating, Coco finished the whole plate of french fries. And the burger really was delicious.

"I told you you would love this place," said Charlie.

Afterwards, Coco had no energy. She didn't feel like running. Instead, she went home and played a computer game. Plop, she fell fast asleep right on the keyboard.

Weeks passed. Coco was running less often and eating at Cheetah Queen more often. Everyone was going to Cheetah Queen—even Coco's mom and dad. Their whole family went for dinner twice a week.

Little by little, Coco noticed that her "Born to Run" shirt was getting tight. It hardly fit over her head.

One day at school, two cheetahs pointed at Coco and laughed. "Fatty," one called her.

"Piglet," the other giggled.

"Little Hippo," they grinned.

Coco felt really sad. She tried to forget about it, but all day long, she heard "Fatty" and "Piglet" and "Little Hippo" inside her head.

That afternoon after track practice, Mr. Phil came over to Coco.

"Coco, I've been meaning to talk with you. Is something wrong?" asked Mr. Phil.

"Nope," she answered. "Everything's fine."

"You haven't been running much, have you?"

"I've missed… a few times," Coco answered slowly.

"A few?" Mr. Phil raised his eyebrows.

"Well, I used to run every evening after dinner, but lately I've been much too tired."

"I can see you haven't been training, Coco," Mr. Phil told her. "I should have said something sooner."

"You're not throwing me off the team, are you?" Coco asked.

"No," said Mr. Phil. "But I am clocking speed today. We're having another practice run to prepare for the Jungle Race judges."

"Clocking speed. A practice run. Not today," a worried Coco thought.

Mr. Phil blew his whistle. "Line up, team. Starting positions please."

When he blew his whistle again, Coco began to run, but something was very wrong. She was running as hard as she could, but the finish line looked so far away. Her legs felt weak, and she was out of breath. She kept trying to run faster, but it was no use. She watched as all the other cheetahs passed her by. Turning her head, she saw no one behind her. How could that be happening?

"It must be a bad dream. I'll wake up soon," Coco thought, rubbing her eyes.

But when the race was over, Kevin had come in first. Mr. Phil read out the times, and sure enough, Coco was the slowest. She didn't need to hear the speeds to know that. She had barely made it to the finish line.

"I've lost my speed," thought Coco, as she tried to catch her breath. Tears rolled down her cheeks.

All the other cheetahs were leaving the track. "Coco, please come here," Mr. Phil called.

As she walked over, her legs were aching, and she still felt out of breath. Mr. Phil got her some water.

"I've lost my speed," she said sadly. "I used to be the fastest, and now I am the slowest. I'll never represent our school at the Jungle Races."

"Coco, we can't change what happened today, but there is something you can do." Mr. Phil said. "You've got to be honest with the most important person in your life—yourself. Now, think about it. Are you eating properly?"

"Not exactly," said Coco. "It all started the day I broke the track record."

Coco told Mr. Phil all about the chocolate cake and Cheetah Queen and how tired she had been lately.

"Little Speedy, I still believe in you," he told Coco.

"I'm not speedy anymore. You should call me Slowpoke."

Mr. Phil took out a photo and showed it to Coco. "This used to be me."

"But the cheetah in that picture is huge," said Coco.

"I didn't eat properly," Mr. Phil explained, "and I didn't exercise. I was always tired, so I just sat and watched television."

"Really?" said Coco.

"Really," said Mr. Phil. "I felt like you do, Coco, and I made up my mind to change. You can change, too. You have to promise yourself that you'll get fit. That means exercising and following a healthy eating plan."

Coco nodded.

"No more junk food, no more Cheetah Queen." Mr. Phil smiled. "Tomorrow, we begin your fitness program."

"What about my parents?" Coco asked. "We go to Cheetah Queen for dinner a few times a week."

"Well, I think it is time I talked with them," said Mr. Phil.

"Thanks, Mr. Phil," said Coco. She was starting to feel better already.

That evening, Coco's mom said, "Mr. Phil called me at work."

"Mr. Phil called me, too," said Dad. "He told us the problem, Coco, and I am afraid that we've been part of it."

"I threw out all the sugary snacks," said Mom, proudly.

"Oh, no," said Chaz.

"They're not good for any of us. And for dinner tonight, we're having a salad, fish, broccoli, and brown rice—and fresh fruit for dessert," said Coco's mom.

Dinner was delicious. "I almost forgot how good healthy food can taste," Chaz said.

"Thanks for a great dinner, Mom," said Coco. "Do you need help with the dishes?"

"No, you go on and finish your homework."

After she finished her homework, Coco looked at her "Born to Run" shirt. "Someday you'll fit better again," she said.

Coco's mom knocked on her door. "Would you like to go for a bike ride with me?"

"I didn't know you liked riding bikes, Mom."

"I used to. I just brought my bike up from the basement and dusted it off," Mom answered proudly.

Coco and her mom got on their bicycles and started pedaling. They came to a large hill. Coco's legs were not strong anymore, and pedaling uphill was rough. She found herself out of breath, and her mom was huffing and puffing, too.

"Wow," Mom panted, "I'm really out of shape!"

The next day after school, Coco went straight to the gym to see Mr. Phil.

"My mom and I went for a bike ride yesterday. Going uphill was so hard!"

"It will get easier as you become fit," promised Mr. Phil. "Let's get started by doing some stretches."

Mr. Phil showed Coco some basic stretches and then put on some peppy music.

"Now it's time to do some aerobic exercise to make your heart strong. Keep running in place," he said, "and then add some jumping jacks."

"1, 2, 3, 4, 5, 6, 7, 8, 9, 10," counted Coco, as she followed Mr. Phil.

"Now some strength training," said Mr. Phil. "We've got to get your body strong again." Mr. Phil showed Coco how to do leg lifts. "Up and down," he said.

Coco could only do three leg lifts on each side.

Mr. Phil said, "You'll see. In no time at all, you'll be doing more. As you keep exercising, you'll get stronger and stronger."

Mr. Phil showed Coco how to do sit-ups, and she did five. Next, it was onto the chinning bar. Coco was so tired that she could barely lift herself once. They ended with some more stretches.

"Good job, Little Speedy," Mr. Phil winked. "Believe in yourself. I certainly believe in you."

Coco wanted to believe that she would be Little Speedy again, but she still had her doubts.

As she headed out of the gym, she nearly bumped into Kevin. "Hey, Slowpoke, it looks like it will be me going to the Jungle Races, not you," he teased.

"Don't count on it."

"Well, the judges are coming in ten weeks to see who will represent our school. Just ten weeks, Little Not-So-Speedy."

"Your backpack is open," said Coco.

Kevin looked over his shoulder.

"Made you look," said Coco. She walked away, smiling to herself.

That evening, Coco ran for the first time in weeks. Inside her head, she kept saying, "I believe in myself." She noticed that she wasn't as out of breath as she had been in the gym, and she felt like her legs were gaining strength.

"Exercising really works," she said. "I have energy for the first time in a long time!"

From then on, Coco ran every day. She never made an excuse. And she stuck to her eating plan. She never skipped breakfast. She usually had cereal with berries and low-fat milk or wheat toast and yogurt with orange juice. She ate smaller portions of foods and fruit and vegetables as snacks. She drank lots of water instead of soda.

Mr. Phil and Coco worked out three times a week on stretching, aerobics, and strength training. Some nights, Coco and her mom rode their bikes. Going uphill was getting easier and easier. Coco wasn't out of breath anymore, and her mom was getting in shape, too.

One afternoon, Coco noticed a big red circle around the next day on the gym calendar. She couldn't believe how quickly time had passed. The Jungle Race judges were coming!

Coco had become much stronger. She could run in place longer. She could do fifty leg lifts on each side. She was up to thirty sit-ups, and she could chin herself twenty-five times.

She was running faster, too. On practice runs, she usually came in third, and on the last practice run, she had come in second.

Still, Kevin was always first. "How can I beat Kevin?" she wondered.

She was thinking about the race as she walked out of the gym.

"Coco," a voice called out.

It was Kevin. "I was hoping I would see you. I didn't mean to call you all those names. That was mean of me, and I wanted to make it up to you so I got you something."

"A present for me?" Coco was surprised.

"A sort of can-we-be-friends present," said Kevin.

"Thanks," said Coco. She looked at the large, white box that Kevin was holding out.

Kevin walked away. "Hope you like it," he said.

Coco opened the box. Inside was a big cake covered with chocolate frosting.

Just then Charlie walked by. "What's that?"

Coco rolled her eyes. "A present from Kevin. I was just thinking that I couldn't win the race, but I might come in second. But you know what?"

"No, what?" asked Charlie.

"Kevin must think I can win. He gave me this cake to slow me down. He wants me to eat the cake and let the sugar sap my energy."

"I think you can win, too," said Charlie.

Coco dumped the cake in the trash can. Charlie clapped.

"Oh, did I tell you?" said Charlie. "I won't be going to Cheetah Queen anymore either. I have nine cavities, and the dentist said they're from all the soda I've been drinking."

Coco giggled. It sure felt good to laugh.

The next morning, the Jungle Race judges arrived. The stands were filled. Coco saw her mom and dad waving to her.

"Cheetahs, take your places," boomed the head judge. He blew his whistle. It was much louder than Mr. Phil's whistle.

Wearing her "Born to Run" shirt, Coco took her place at the starting line.

"When I blow the whistle again, cheetahs, take off," said the judge. He blew the whistle even louder.

Coco took off, leaving the other cheetahs way behind—all except Kevin. He was out in front. As she came up behind him, Coco felt as if all four of her feet were lifting off the ground at the same time.

Just then, Kevin took a gigantic leap forward. Coco pushed herself harder, but Kevin was way ahead. She watched as Kevin took an even bigger lead.

"Oh, forget it," she thought. "What was I thinking? How can I possibly beat him?" And then, as she was running, Coco remembered all her hard work.

In a flash, she remembered how hard it had been for her to do even five sit-ups and three leg lifts. She thought of how difficult it had been to go uphill the first night she went bike riding with her mom.

"There is no way I'm giving up now," Coco said aloud. "I've worked too hard for this."

Her legs felt strong beneath her. She rounded the bend in the track and zoomed forward at lightning speed. Kevin was just a few feet ahead, and he dashed faster and faster.

As she was running, Coco remembered all the mean names, the teasing, and the cake. She picked up speed, repeating to herself, "I believe in myself, I believe in myself."

Kevin and Coco were neck and neck. He turned his head and saw Coco running right beside him.

"How did you catch up to me?" he asked, totally stunned.

Coco had so much energy and strength that she nearly flew through the air, shouting, "Bye-bye, Kevin. Now you see me, now you don't." She blasted forward, leaving Kevin in the dust.

The crowd chanted "Coco, Coco, Coco," as she zoomed across the finish line.

Coco had won.

"It's official," said the head judge. "Coco will be your representative to the Jungle Races." He shook Coco's hand.

Charlie jumped down from the stands and hugged Coco. Her mom, her dad, and Chaz joined in.

As Kevin walked by, Coco put out her hand. "You ran a great race, Kevin."

"But you ran a better one. I guess you really are Little Speedy." They shook hands.

Mr. Phil came over with a big smile. "Congratulations, Little Speedy!" he said.

Coco smiled back at him. "Thanks for believing in me."

"What's more important," said Mr. Phil, "is that you believed in yourself."